The Lady Rustic

ALEXANDER PUSHKIN

translated by
Margaret
Sutherland Edwards

first published in
1892

In one of our distant
provinces was
the estate of Ivan
Berestoff. As a youth
he served in the
guards, but having
left the army early
in 1797 he retired
to his country seat
and there remained.

He married a wife from among the poor nobility, and when she died in childbed he happened to be detained on farming business in one of his distant fields. His daily occupations soon brought him consolation. He built a house on his own plan, set up his own cloth factory, became his own auditor and accountant, and began to think himself the cleverest fellow in the whole district. The neighbours who used to come to him upon a visit and bring their families and dogs took good care not to contradict him. His work-a-day dress was a short coat of velveteen; on holidays he wore a frock-coat of cloth from his own factory. His accounts took most of his time, and he read nothing but the *Senatorial News*. On the whole, though he was considered proud, he was not disliked. The only person who could never get on with him was his nearest neighbour, Gregory Muromsky. A true Russian *barin*, a gentleman who had squandered in Moscow a large part of his estate, and having lost his wife as well as his money he had retired to his sole remaining property, and there continued his extragavance but in a different way. He set up an English garden on which he spent nearly all the income he had left. His grooms wore English liveries. An English governess taught his daughter. He farmed his land upon the

English system. But foreign farming grows no Russian corn.

So, in spite of his retirement, the income of Gregory Muromsky did not increase. Even in the country he had a faculty for making new debts. But he was no fool, people said, for was he not the first landowner in all that province to mortgage his property to the government--a process then generally believed to be one of great complexity and risk? Among his detractors Berestoff, a thorough hater of innovation, was the most severe. In speaking of his neighbour's Anglo-mania he could scarcely keep his feelings under control, and missed no opportunity for criticism. To some compliment from a visitor to his estate he would answer, with a knowing smile:

"Yes, my farming is not like that of Gregory Muromsky. I can't afford to ruin my land on the English system, but I am satisfied to escape starvation on the Russian."

Obliging neighbours reported these and other jokes to Gregory, with additions and commentaries of their own. The Anglo-maniac was as irritable as a journalist under this criticism, and wrathfully referred to his critic as a bumpkin and a bear.

Relations were

thus strained when Berestoff's son came home. Having finished his university career, he wanted to go into the army; but his father objected. For the civil service young Berestoff had no taste. Neither would yield, so young Alex took up the life of a country gentleman, and to be ready for emergencies cultivated a moustache. He was really a handsome fellow, and it would indeed have been a pity never to pinch his fine figure into a military uniform, and instead of displaying his broad shoulders on horseback to round them over an office desk. Ever foremost in the hunting-field, and a straight rider, it was quite clear, declared the neighbours, that he could never make a good official. The shy young ladies glanced and the bold stared at him in admiration; but he took no notice of them, and each could only attribute his indifference to some prior attachment. In fact, there was in private circulation, copied from an envelope in his handwriting, this address:

A. N. P.,   Care
of Akulina Petrovna
Kurotchkina,
Opposite Alexeieff
Monastery.

Those readers who
have not seen our
country life can
hardly realize the
charm of these
provincial girls.
Breathing pure air
under the shadow of

their apple trees, their only knowledge of the world is drawn from books. In solitude and unrestrained, their feelings and their passions develop early to a degree unknown to the busier beauties of our towns. For them the tinkling of a bell is an event, a drive into the nearest town an epoch, and a chance visit a long, sometimes an everlasting remembrance. At their oddities he may laugh who will, but superficial sneers cannot impair their real merits--their individuality, which, so says Jean Paul, is a necessary element of greatness. The women in large towns may be better educated, but the levelling influence of the world soon makes all women as much alike as their own head-dresses.

Let not this be regarded as condemnation. Still as an ancient writer says *nota nostra manet*: the fact remains.

It may be imagined what an impression Alex made on our country misses. He was the first gloomy

and disenchanted
hero they had ever
beheld; the first who
ever spoke to them
of vanished joys
and blighted past.
Besides, he wore
a black ring with a
death's head on it. All
this was quite a new
thing in that province,
and the young ladies
all went crazy.

But she in whose
thoughts he dwelt

most deeply was Lisa, the daughter of Gregory Muromsky. Their fathers did not visit, so she had never seen Alex, who was the sole topic of conversation among her young neighbours. She was just seventeen, with dark eyes lighting up her pretty face. An only, and consequently a spoilt child, full of life and mischief, she was the delight of her father, and the distraction of her governess, Miss Jackson, a prim spinster in the forties, who powdered her face and blackened her eyebrows, read Pamela twice a year, drew a salary of 2,000 rubles, and was nearly bored to death in barbarous Russia.

Lisa's maid Nastia was older, but quite as flighty as her mistress, who was very fond of her, and had her as confidante in all her secrets and as fellow-conspirator in her mischief.

In fact, no leading lady played half such an important part in French tragedy as was played by Nastia in the village.

Said Nastia, while dressing her young lady:

"May I go to-day and visit a friend?"

"Yes. Where?"

"To the Berestoff's. It is the cook's namesday. He called yesterday to ask us to dinner."

"Then," said Lisa, "the masters quarrel and the servants entertain one another."

"And what does that matter to us?" said Nastia. "I belong to you and not to your father. You have not quarrelled with young Berestoff yet. Let the old people fight if they please."

"Nastia! try and see

Alexei Berestoff. Come back and tell me all about him."

Nastia promised; Lisa spent the whole day impatiently waiting for her. In the evening she returned.

"Well, Lisa!" she said, as she entered the room.

"I have seen young Berestoff. I had a

good look at him. We spent the whole day together."

"How so? tell me all about it."

"Certainly? We started, I and Anissia----"

"Yes, yes, I know! What then?"

"I would rather tell you in proper order.

We were just in time for dinner; the room was quite full. There were the Zaharievskys, the steward's wife and daughters, the Shlupinskys----"

"Yes, yes! And Berestoff?"

"Wait a bit. We sat down to dinner. The steward's wife had the seat of honour; I sat next to her, and her daughters were huffy; but what do I care!"

"Oh, Nastia! How tiresome you are with these everlasting details!"

"How impatient you are! Well, then we rose from table--we had been sitting for about three hours and it was a splendid dinner-party, blue, red and striped creams--then we went into the garden to play at kiss-in-the-ring when the young gentleman appeared."

"Well, is it true? Is he so handsome?"

"Wonderfully handsome! I may say beautiful. Tall, stately, with a lovely colour."

"Really! I thought his face was pale. Well, how did he strike you--Was he melancholy and thoughtful?"

"Oh, no! I never saw such a mad fellow. He took it into his head to join us at kiss-in-the-ring." "He played at kiss-in-the-ring! It is impossible."

"No, it's very possible; and what more do you think? When he caught any one he kissed her." "Of course you may tell lies if you like, Nastia."

"As you please, miss, only I am not lying. I could scarcely get away from him. Indeed he spent the whole day with us."

"Why do people say then that he is in love and looks at nobody?"

"I am sure I don't know, miss. He looked too much at me and Tania too, the steward's daughter, and at Pasha too. In fact, he neglected nobody. He is such a wild fellow!"

"This is surprising; and what do the servants

say about him?”

“They say he is a splendid gentleman--so kind, so lively! He has only one fault: he is too fond of the girls. But I don't think that is such a great fault. He will get steadier in time.”

“How I should like to see him,” said Lisa, with a sigh.

"And why can't you? Tugilovo is only a mile off. Take a walk in that direction, or a ride, and you are sure to meet him. He shoulders his gun and goes shooting every morning."

"No, it would never do. He would think I was running after him. Besides, our fathers have quarrelled, so he and I could hardly set up a friendship. Oh, Nastia! I know what I'll do. I will dress up like a peasant."

"That will do. Put on a coarse chemise and a *sarafan*, and set out boldly for Tugilovo. Berestoff will never miss you I promise you."

"I can talk like a peasant splendidly.

Oh, Nastia, dear Nastia, what a happy thought!" and Lisa went to bed resolved to carry out her plan. Next day she made her preparations. She went to the market for some coarse linen, some dark blue stuff, and some brass buttons, and out of these Nastia and she cut a chemise and a *sarafan*. All the maid-servants were set down to sew, and by evening everything was ready.

As she tried on her new costume before the glass, Lisa said to herself that she had never looked so nice. Then she began to rehearse her meeting with Alex. First she gave him a low bow as she passed along, then she continued to nod her head like a mandarin. Next she addressed him in a peasant *patois*, simpering and shyly hiding her face behind her sleeve. Nastia gave the performance her full approval. But there was one difficulty. She tried to cross the yard barefooted, but the grass stalks pricked her tender feet and the gravel caused intolerable pain. Nastia again came to the rescue.

She took the measure of Lisa's foot and hurried across the fields to the herdsman Trophim, of whom she ordered a pair of bark shoes.

The next morning before daylight Lisa awoke. The whole household was still asleep. Nastia was at the gate waiting for the herdsman; soon the sound of his horn drew near, and the village herd straggled past the Manor gates. After them came Trophim, who, as he passed, handed to Nastia a little pair of speckled bark shoes, and received a ruble.

Lisa, who had quietly donned her peasant dress, whispered

to Nastia her last instructions about Miss Jackson; then she went through the kitchen, out of the back door, into the open field, then she began to run.

Dawn was breaking, and the rows of golden clouds stood like courtiers waiting for their monarch. The clear sky, the fresh morning air, the dew, the breeze and singing of the birds filled Lisa's heart with child-like joy.

Fearing to meet with some acquaintance, she did nor walk but flew. As she drew near the wood where lay the boundary of her father's property she slackened her pace. It was here she was to meet Alex. Her heart beat violently, she knew not why. The terrors of our youthful escahades are their chief charm.

Lisa stepped forward into the darkness of the wood; its hollow echoes bade her welcome. Her buoyant spirits gradually gave place to meditation. She thought--but who shall truly tell the thoughts of sweet seventeen in a wood, alone, at six o'clock on a spring morning?

And as she walked in meditation under the shade of lofty trees, suddenly a beautiful pointer began to bark at her. Lisa cried out with fear, and at the same moment a voice exclaimed, "*Tout beau Shogar, ici,*" and a young sportsman stepped from behind the bushes. "Don't be afraid, my dear, he won't bite."

Lisa had already recovered from her fright, and instantly took advantage of the situation.

"It's all very well, sir," she said, with assumed timidity and shyness, "I am afraid of him, he seems such a savage creature, and may fly at me again."

Alex, whom the reader has already recognised, looked steadily at the young peasant. "I will escort you, if you are afraid; will you allow me to walk by your side?"

"Who is to prevent you?" replied Lisa. "A freeman can do as he likes, and the road is public!"

"Where do you come from?"

"From Prilutchina;
I am the daughter
of Yassili, the
blacksmith, and
I am looking for
mushrooms." She was
carrying a basket
suspended from her
shoulders by a cord.

"And you, Sir; are you
from Tugilovo?"

"Exactly, I am the young gentleman's valet" (he wished to equalize their ranks). But Lisa looked at him and laughed.

"Ah! you are lying," she said. "I am not a fool. I see you are the master himself."

"What makes you think so?"

"Everything."

"Still----?"

"How can one help it. You are not dressed like a servant. You speak differently. You even call your dog in a foreign tongue."

Lisa charmed him more and more every moment. Accustomed to be unceremonious with pretty country girls, he tried to kiss her, but Lisa jumped aside, and suddenly assumed so distant and severe an air that though it amused him he did not attempt any further familiarities.

"If you wish to remain friends," she said, with dignity, "do not forget yourself."

"Who has taught you

this wisdom?" asked
Alex, with a laugh.
"Can it be my little
friend Nastia, your
mistress's maid? So
this is how civilization
spreads."

Lisa felt she had
almost betrayed
herself, and said,
"Do you think I have
never been up to
the Manor House? I
have seen and heard
more than you think.

Still, chattering here with you won't get me mushrooms. You go that way, Sir; I'll go the other, begging your pardon;" and Lisa made as if to depart, but Alex held her by the hand.

"What is your name, my dear?"

"Akulina," she said, struggling to get her fingers free. "Let me go, Sir, it is time for me to be home."

"Well, my friend Akulina, I shall certainly call on your father, Yassili, the blacksmith."

"For the Lord's sake don't do that. If they knew at home I had been talking here alone with the young gentleman, I should catch it. My father would beat me within an inch of my life."

"Well, I must see you again."

"I will come again some other day for mushrooms."

"When?"

"Tomorrow, if you like."

"My dear Akulina, I

would kiss you if I dared. Tomorrow, then, at the same time; that is a bargain."

"All right."

"You will not play me false?"

"No."

"Swear it."

"By the Holy Friday,

then, I will come."

The young couple parted. Lisa ran out of the wood across the fields, stole into the garden, and rushed headlong into the farmyard, where Nastia was waiting for her. Then she changed her dress, answering at random the impatient questions of her confidante, and went into the dining-room to find the cloth laid and breakfast ready. Miss Jackson, freshly powdered and Jaced, until she looked like a wine glass, was cutting thin slices of bread and butter. Her father complimented Lisa on her early walk.

"There is no healthier habit," he remarked, "than to rise at daybreak." He quoted from the English papers several cases of longevity, adding that all centenarians had abstained from spirits, and made it a practice to rise at daybreak winter and summer. Lisa did not prove an attentive listener. She was repeating in her mind the details of her morning's interview, and as she recalled Akulina's conversation with the young sportsman her conscience smote her. In vain she assured herself that the bounds of decorum had not been passed. This joke, she argued, could have no evil consequences, but conscience would not be quieted. What most disturbed her was her promise to repeat the meeting.

She half decided not to keep her word, but then Alex, tired of waiting, might go to seek the blacksmiths daughter in the village and find the real Akulina--a stout, pockmarked girl--and so discover the hoax. Alarmed at this she determined to re-enact the part of Akulina. Alex was enchanted. All day he thought about his new acquaintance and at night he dreamt of her. It was scarcely dawn when he was up and dressed. Without waiting even to load his gun he set out followed by the faithful Shogar, and ran to the meeting place. Half an hour passed in undeniable delay. At last he caught a glimpse of a blue *sarafan* among the bushes and rushed to meet dear Akulina. She smiled to see his eagerness; but he saw traces of anxiety and melancholy on her face. He asked her the cause, and she at last confessed. She had been flighty and was very sorry for it. She had meant not to keep her promise, and this meeting at any rate must be the last. She begged him not to seek to continue an acquaintance which could have no good end. All this, of course, was said in peasant dialect; but the thought and feeling struck Alex as unusual in a peasant. In eloquent words he urged her to abandon this cruel resolution. She should have no reason for repentance; he would obey her in everything, if only she would not rob him of his one happiness and let him see her alone three times or even only twice a week. He spoke with passion, and at the moment he was really in love. Lisa listened to him in silence.

"Promise," she said, "to seek no other meetings with me but those which I myself appoint."

He was about to swear by the Holy Friday when she stopped him with a smile.

"I do not want you to swear. Your word is enough."

Then together they wandered talking in the wood, till Lisa said:

"It is time."

They parted; and Alex was left to wonder how in two meetings a simple rustic had gained such influence over him. There was a freshness and novelty about it all that charmed him, and though the conditions she imposed were irksome, the thought of breaking his promise never even entered his mind. After all, in spite of his fatal ring and the mysterious correspondence, Alex was a kind and affectionate youth, with a pure heart still capable of innocent enjoyment. Did I consult only my own wishes I should dwell at length on the meetings of these young people, their growing love, their mutual trust, and all they did and all they said. But my pleasure I know would not be shared by the majority of my readers; so for their sake I will omit them. I will only say that in a brief two months Alex was already madly in love, and Lisa, though more reticent than he was, not indifferent. Happy in the present they took little thought for the future. Visions of indissoluble ties flitted not seldom through the minds of both. But neither mentioned them. For Alex, however strong his attachment to Akulina, could not forget the social distance that was between them, while Lisa, knowing the enmity between their fathers, dared not count on their becoming reconciled. Besides, her vanity was stimulated by the vague romantic hope of at last seeing the lord of Tugilovo at the feet of the daughter of a village blacksmith. Suddenly something happened which came near to change the course of their true love. One of those cold bright mornings so common in our Russian autumns Ivan Berestoff came a-riding. For all emergencies he brought with him six pointers and a dozen beaters. That same morning Gregory Muromsky, tempted by the fine weather, saddled his English mare and came trotting through his agricultural estates. Nearing the wood he came upon his neighbour proudly seated in the saddle wearing his fur-lined overcoat. Ivan Berestoff was waiting for the hare which the beaters were driving with discordant noises out of the brushwood. If Muromsky could have foreseen this meeting he would have avoided it. But finding himself suddenly within pistol-shot there was no escape. Like a cultivated European gentleman, Muromsky rode up to and addressed his enemy politely. Berestoff answered with the grace of a chained bear dancing to the order of his keeper. At this moment out shot the hare and scudded across the field. Berestoff and his groom shouted to loose the dogs, and started after them full speed. Muromsky's mare took fright and bolted. Her rider, who often boasted of his horsemanship, gave her her head and chuckled inwardly over this opportunity of escaping a disagreeable companion. But the mare coming at a gallop to an unseen ditch swerved.

Muromsky lost his seat, fell rather heavily on the frozen ground, and lay there cursing the animal, which, sobered by the loss of her master, stopped at once. Berestoff galloped to the rescue, asking if Muromsky was hurt. Meanwhile the groom led up the culprit by the bridle. Berestoff helped Muromsky into the saddle and then invited him to his house. Feeling himself under an obligation Muromsky could not refuse, and so Berestoff returned in glory, having killed the hare and bringing home with him his adversary wounded and almost a prisoner of war.

At breakfast the neighbours fell into rather friendly

conversation; Muromsky asked Berestoff to lend him a droshky, or carriage, confessing that his fall made it too painful for him to ride back. Berestoff accompanied him to the outer gate, and before the leavetaking was over Muromsky Had obtained from him a promise to come and bring Alex to a friendly dinner at Prelutchina next day. So this old enmity which seemed before so deeply rooted was on the point of ending because the little mare had taken fright.

Lisa ran to meet her father on his return.

"What has happened, papa?" she asked in astonishment. "Why are you limping?

Where is the mare? Whose droshky is this?”

“My dear, you will never guess;”--and then he told her.

Lisa could not believe her ears. Before she Had time to collect herself she heard that tomorrow both the Berestoffs would come to dinner.

"What do you say?" she exclaimed, turning pale. "The Berestoffs, father and son! Dine with us tomorrow! No, papa, you can do as you please, I certainly do not appear."

"Why? Are you mad? Since when have you become so shy? Have you imbibed hereditary hatred like a heroine of romance? Come, don't be afoot."

"No, papa, nothing on earth shall induce me to meet the Berestoffs."

Her father shrugged his shoulders, and left off arguing. He knew he could not prevail with her by opposition, so he went to bed after his memorable ride. Lisa, too, went to her room, and summoned

Nastia. Long did they discuss the coming visit. What will Alex think on recognising in the cultivated young lady his Akulina? What opinion will he form as to her behaviour and her sense? On the other hand, Lisa was very curious to see how such an unexpected meeting would affect him. Then an idea struck her. She told it to Nastia, and with rejoicing they determined to carry it into effect.

Next morning at breakfast Muromsky asked his daughter whether she still meant to hide from the Berestoffs.

"Papa," she answered, "I will receive them if you wish it, on one condition. However

I may appear before them, whatever I may do, you must promise me not to be angry, and you must show no surprise or disapproval."

"At your tricks again!" exclaimed Muromsky, laughing. "Well, well, I consent; do as you please, my black-eyed mischief." With these words he kissed her forehead, and Lisa ran off to make her preparations.

Punctually at two, six horses, drawing the home-made carriage, drove into the courtyard, and skirted the circle of green turf that formed its centre.

Old Berestoff, helped by two of Muromsky's servants in livery, mounted the steps.

His son followed immediately on horseback, and the two together entered the dining-room, where the table was already laid.

Muromsky gave his guests a cordial welcome, and proposing a tour of inspection of the garden and live stock before dinner, led them along his well-swept gravel paths.

Old Berestoff secretly deplored the time and trouble wasted on such a useless whim as this Anglo-mania, but politeness forbade him to express his feelings.

His son shared neither the disapproval of the careful farmer, nor the enthusiasm of the complacent Anglo-maniac. He impatiently awaited the appearance of his hosts daughter, of whom he had often heard; for, though his heart as we know was no longer free, a young and unknown beauty might still claim his interest.

When they had come back and were all seated in

the drawing-room, the old men talked over bygone days, re-telling the stories of the mess-room, while Alex considered what attitude he should assume towards Lisa. He decided upon a cold preoccupation as most suitable, and arranged accordingly.

The door opened, he turned his head round

with indifference-
-with such proud
indifference--that the
heart of the most
hardened coquette
must have quivered.
Unfortunately there
came in not Lisa but
elderly Miss Jackson,
whitened, laced in,
with downcast eyes
and her little curtsey,
and Alex's magnificent
military movement
failed. Before he
could reassemble

his scattered forces the door opened again and this time entered Lisa. All rose, Muromsky began the introductions, but suddenly stopped and bit his lip. Lisa, his dark Lisa, was painted white up to her ears, and pencilled worse than Miss Jackson herself. She wore false fair ringlets, puffed out like a Louis XIV. wig; her sleeves à *l'imbécille* extended like the hoops of Madame de Pomhadour. Her figure was laced in like a letter X, and all those of her mother's diamonds which had escaped the pawnbroker sparkled on her fingers, neck, and ears. Alex could not discover in this ridiculous young lady his Akulina. His father kissed her hand,

and he, much to his annoyance, had to do the same. As he touched her little white fingers they seemed to tremble. He noticed, too, a tiny foot intentionally displayed and shod in the most coquettish of shoes. This reconciled him a little to the rest of her attire. The white paint and black pencilling--to tell the

truth--in his simplicity
he did not notice
at first, nor indeed
afterwards.

Gregory Muromsky,
remembering his
promise, tried not
to show surprise;
for the rest, he was
so much amused
at his daughter's
mischief, that he could
scarcely keep his
countenance. For the
prim Englishwoman,

however, it was no laughing matter. She guessed that the white and black paint had been abstracted from her drawer, and a red patch of indignation shone through the artificial whiteness of her face. Flaming glances shot from her eyes at the young rogue, who, reserving all explanation for the future, pretended not to notice them. They sat down to table, Alex continuing his performance as an absent-minded pensive man. Lisa was all affectation. She minced her words, drawled, and would speak only in French. Her father glanced at her from time to time, unable to divine her object, but he thought it all a great joke. The Englishwoman fumed, but said nothing. Ivan Berestoff alone felt at his ease. He ate for two, drank his fill, and as the meal went on became more and more friendly, and laughed louder and louder.

At last they rose from the table. The guests departed and Muromsky gave vent to his mirth and curiosity.

"What made you play such tricks upon them?" he inquired. "Do you know, Lisa, that white paint really becomes you? I do not wish to pry into the secrets of a lady's toilet, but if I were you I should always paint, not too much, of course, but a little."

Lisa was delighted with her success. She

kissed her father, promised to consider his suggestion, and ran off to propitiate the enraged Miss Jackson, whom she could scarcely prevail upon to open the door and hear her excuses.

Lisa was ashamed, she said, to show herself before the visitors--such a blackamoor. She had not dared to ask; she knew dear kind Miss Jackson would forgive her.

Miss Jackson, persuaded that her pupil had not meant to ridicule her, became pacified, kissed Lisa, and in token of forgiveness presented her with a little pot of English white, which the latter, with expressions of deep gratitude, accepted.

Next morning, as the reader will have guessed, Lisa hastened to the meeting in the wood.

"You were yesterday at our master's, sir?" she began to Alex. "What did you think of our young lady?"

Alex answered that he had not observed her.

"That is a pity."

"Why?"

"Because I wanted to ask you if what they say is true."

"What do they say?"

"That I resemble our young lady; do you think so?"

"What nonsense, she

is a deformity beside you!"

"Oh! Sir, it is a sin of you to say so. Our young lady is so fair, so elegant! How can I vie with her?"

Alex vowed that she was prettier than all imaginable fair young ladies, and to appease her thoroughly, began describing her young lady so funnily that

Lisa burst into a hearty laugh.

"Still," she said, with a sigh, "though she may be ridiculous, yet by her side I am an illiterate fool."

"Well, that *is* a thing to worry yourself about. If you like I will teach you to read at once."

"Are you in earnest,

shall I really try?"

"If you like, my darling, we will begin at once."

They sat down. Alex produced a pencil and note-book, and Akulina proved astonishingly quick in learning the alphabet. Alex wondered at her intelligence. At their next meeting she wished to learn to write. The pencil at first would not obey her, but in a few minutes she could trace the letters pretty well.

"How wonderfully we get on, faster than by the Lancaster method."

Indeed, at the third lesson Akulina could read words of even three syllables,

and the intelligent
remarks with which
she interrupted
the lessons fairly
astonished Alex.
As for writing she
covered a whole page
with aphorisms, taken
from the story she
had been reading.
A week passed and
they had begun a
correspondence. Their
post-office was the
trunk of an old oak,
and Nastia secretly

played the part of postman. Thither Alex would bring his letters, written in a large round hand, and there he found the letters of his beloved scrawled on coarse blue paper. Akulina's style was evidently improving, and her mind clearly was developing under cultivation.

Meanwhile the new-made

acquaintance between Berestoff and Muromsky grew stronger, soon it became friendship. Muromsky often reflected that on the death of old Berestoff his property would come to Alex, who would then be one of the richest landowners in that province. Why should he not marry Lisa? Old Berestoff, on the other hand, though he looked on his neighbour as a lunatic, did not deny that he possessed many excellent qualities, among them a certain cleverness. Muromsky was related to Count Pronsky, a distinguished and influential man. The count might be very useful to Alex, and Muromsky (so thought Berestoff) would probably be glad to marry his daughter so well. Both the old men pondered all this so thoroughly that at last they broached the subject, confabulated, embraced, and severally began a plan of campaign. Muromsky foresaw one difficulty--how to persuade his Lisa to make the better acquaintance of

Alex, whom she had never seen since the memorable dinner. They hardly seemed to suit each other well. At any rate Alex had not renewed his visit. Whenever old Berestoff called Lisa made a point of retreating to her own room.

"But," thought Muromsky, "if Alex called every day Lisa

could not help falling in love with him. That is the way to manage it. Time will settle everything."

Berestoff troubled himself less about his plans. That same evening he called his son into his study, lit his pipe, and, after a short silence, began:

"You have not spoken about the army

lately, Alex. Has the Hussar uniform lost its attraction for you?"

"No, father," he replied respectfully. "I know you do not wish me to join the Hussars. It is my duty to consult your wishes."

"I am pleased to find you such an obedient son, still I do not wish to force your inclinations. I will not insist upon your entering the Civil Service at once; and in the meantime I mean to marry you."

"To whom, father?" exclaimed his astonished son.

"To Lisa Muromsky; she is good enough for any one, isn't she?"

"Father, I did not think of marrying just yet."

"Perhaps not, but I have thought about it for you."

"As you please, but I don't care about Lisa Muromsky at all."

"You will care about her afterwards. You will get used to her, and you will learn to love her."

"I feel I could not make her happy."

"You need not trouble yourself about that. All you have to do is to respect the wishes of your father."

"I do not wish to marry, and I won't."

"You shall marry or I will curse you; and, by Heaven, I will sell and squander my property, and not leave you a farthing! I will give you three days for reflection, and, in the meanwhile, do not dare to show your face in my presence."

Alex knew that when his father took a thing into his head nothing could knock it out again; but then Alex was as obstinate as his father. He went to his room and there reflected upon the limits of parental authority, on Lisa Muromsky, his father's threat to make him a beggar, and finally he thought of Akulina.

For the first time he clearly saw how much he loved her. The romantic idea of marrying a peasant

girl and working for
a living came into his
mind; and the more
he thought of it, the
more he approved
it. Their meetings in
the wood had been
stopped of late by the
wet weather.

He wrote to Akulina
in the roundest hand
and the maddest
style, telling her of
his impending ruin,
and asking her to be

his wife. He took the letter at once to the tree trunk, dropped it in, and went much satisfied with himself to bed.

Next morning, firm in resolution, he started early to call on Muromsky and explain the situation. He meant to win him over by appealing to his generosity.

"Is Mr. Muromsky at home?" he asked reining up his horse at the porch.

"No, sir, Mr. Muromsky went out early this morning."

How provoking, thought Alex.

"Well, is Miss Lisa at home?"

"Yes, sir."

And throwing the reins to the footman, Alex leapt from his horse and entered unannounced.

"It will soon be over," he thought, going towards the drawing-room. "I will explain to Miss Muromsky herself." He entered ... and was transfixed. Lisa!... no, Akulina, dear, dark Akulina, wearing no *sarafan* but a white morning frock, sat by the window reading his letter. So intent was she upon it that she did not hear him enter. Alex could not repress a cry of delight. Lisa started, raised her hand, cried out, and attempted to run away. He rushed to stop her. "Akulina! Akulina!" Lisa tried to free herself.

"Mais laissez moi donc, Monsieur! mais êtes vous fou?" she repeated, turning away.

"Akulina! my darling Akulina!" he repeated, kissing her hand.

Miss Jackson, who was an eye-witness of this scene, knew not what to think. The door opened and Gregory Muromsky entered.

"Ah!" cried he, "you seem to have settled things between you."...

The reader will excuse me the unnecessary trouble of winding up.

THE END

ABOUT THE AUTHOR

Alexander Pushkin was a poet, playwright, and novelist of the Romantic era who is considered by many to be the greatest Russian poet and the founder of modern Russian literature. He died after being shot in a duel with a Frenchman who had wooed his wife.

ABOUT THE COVER

The image on the cover is adapted from a poster for the 1925 silent film, "The Big Parade," starring John Gilbert and Renée Adorée.

MORE BOOKS AT:
superlargeprint.com

KEEP ON READING!

This book is set in a font designed by
Abelardo Gonzalez called OpenDyslexic.

ISBN 198112277X
ISBN 978-1981122776

Printed in Great Britain
by Amazon

60493195R00077